Family Story Collection

There's Strength in Numbers

STORIES ABOUT TEAMWORK AND DETERMINATION

Book Eleven

INCLUDING CHARACTERS FROM YOUR FAVORITE · PIXAR FILMS

Printed in China
First Edition
1 3 5 7 9 10 8 6 4 2

ISBN 0-7868-3535-4

For more Disney Press fun, visit www.disneybooks.com

Book Eleven

There's Strength
in Numbers

STORIES ABOUT TEAMWORK AND DETERMINATION

Introduction

Learning to cooperate, to trust others, and to work together are key lessons in every person's life. While many can accomplish a lot on their own, a person's potential is amplified when combined with the strengths and talents of others. Through teamwork, momentous tasks may be undertaken, and success realized.

In "Pulling Together," Buzz and the toys work together to save their friend, Woody. Only when they combine their talents can they overcome the obstacles that stand in their way. Flik, in "The Ants' Only Chance," sees that he can do more to battle the grasshoppers with the help of friends, than he can do by himself. The ants have a powerful weapon that the grasshoppers don't— teamwork!

Pulling Together

from *Toy Story 2*

Anything is possible when you're part of a good team.

oody had been toynapped by Al McWhiggin, the owner of Al's Toy Barn, and his friends were ready to rush to his rescue. "Woody once risked his life to save me," Buzz Lightyear announced to the rest of the toys. "I can't call myself his friend if I'm not willing to do the same."

"I'm coming with you," Slinky Dog told Buzz.

Rex the dinosaur and Hamm the piggy bank agreed to help, too.

That night, the toys sneaked out of the house and onto the roof. It was a long way down. Luckily, Slinky Dog was there. He helped the others get down safely.

They bravely made their way across town and soon spotted Al's Toy Barn. There was just one problem: it stood on the other side of a wide, busy street.

"There must be a safe way across," Buzz said. Then, he had a great idea. Some orange traffic cones were nearby. Buzz told the others to put them over their heads. They rushed safely across the lanes of traffic, but caused a major traffic jam in the process.

Finally, the toys made it to the store. Woody wasn't there, and Al was on the phone. They overheard him say he was selling

Woody to a toy museum! The toys just *had* to get to Woody, so they followed Al to his apartment building. The toys broke through an air vent that led to Al's apartment and climbed up through it. It was hard work, but they helped one another all the way.

They tried to convince Woody to come home, but he didn't want to leave. The toys finally gave up. It was then that Woody realized how much he missed home. He

called out to his friends, but it was too late. Al came into the room and packed Woody and the others into a special carrying case.

However, Buzz heard Woody's call, and the toys ran to the elevator to follow him. Just then, Zurg, Buzz's archenemy, appeared! Zurg was very strong. He began to attack the toys. But then Rex spun around, accidentally knocking Zurg right down the elevator shaft. Rex had saved them!

But they still had to save Woody. The friends followed Al outside. Then they watched in horror as he climbed into his car and drove toward the airport.

"How are we going to save Woody now?" Rex cried.

Suddenly, the toys noticed a pizza truck parked nearby.

The toys hopped into the truck. Buzz climbed behind the steering wheel. "Slink, you take the pedals," he instructed. "Rex, you navigate. Hamm, operate the levers and knobs."

Everyone had a job. The toys did as they were told, and the truck started! They took off after Woody.

The toys were excited. Each of them was doing his part to make the rescue mission work. They made a great team. Nothing could stop them from saving Woody now!

The Ants' Only Chance

from *A Bug's Life*

The only failure is the failure to try.

Princess Dot hid behind some grass as two big, mean grasshoppers walked by. They were talking about their leader's evil plan to attack the ant colony. "After we steal their food, he'll squash the Queen to show who's boss," one explained. "She's dead; they cry, 'boohoo'; we go home; end of story." The other grasshopper snickered.

Dot gasped. The ants needed help—and quick! She knew that the only one who could save them was her friend Flik. But the colony had banished him for good.

Poor Flik! All he wanted to do was help make life easier for the ants. He invented all kinds of new gadgets. But most of them didn't work well. And lately his ideas had gotten the colony into big trouble.

First, his grain-picking machine had destroyed the ants' food offering to the grasshoppers. Then, when he promised to find warriors to fight the grasshoppers, he had accidentally returned with circus performers instead. The colony was so fed up with Flik that they had sent him and his circus bugs away.

But Dot had always believed in Flik. She raced to find him and the circus bugs. She knew they could help.

When she found them, she quickly explained what she had overheard from the grasshoppers.

"We have to do something!" cried Rosie the spider.

"I know!" exclaimed Gypsy the moth. "The bird."

Flik's latest invention was an enormous mechanical bird that was meant to scare the grasshoppers away.

"The bird! That's brilliant," said Slim the walking stick.

But then, to everyone's surprise, Flik shook his head and said, "The bird won't work. The colony is right. I just make things worse. That bird is a guaranteed failure. Just like me."

Flik used to believe in himself and his inventions, but his confidence was shaken. His friends tried to boost Flik's spirits and encourage him to try.

"We'll follow you into the battle," Francis the ladybug assured him.

"We believe in you," said Manny the praying mantis.

Still, Flik was afraid his invention wouldn't work. He just couldn't risk failing again.

Then Dot handed Flik a small rock. "Pretend it's a seed," she said with a wink.

A few days earlier, Dot had complained to Flik about being too small to fly. Flik had held a rock and asked her to pretend it was a seed. "Everything that made the giant tree is already contained in this tiny, little seed," he told her.

Flik looked at the rock and smiled.

"Thanks, Dot," he said.

Even though defeating the grasshoppers seemed like an impossible task, Flik knew he had to try. "All right," Flick said with resolve. "Let's do it!"

Now that his determination was back, Flik was ready to lead everyone into battle. Surely, they could accomplish anything they wanted to by working together.